GOOD FOR YOU, GRISHA!

Teaching Kids Ways to Cope

By Karen Westhoven
Illustrated by
Mary Gregg Byrne

CRNE PRESS

Good for You, Grisha! Teaching Kids Ways to Cope

Copyright © 2012 by Karen Westhoven
Illustrated by Mary Gregg Byrne
Illustrations created with watercolors
Layout and cover design by Jacqueline L. Challiss Hill

Printed in the United States of America

Summary: A young boy realizes he isn't that different from his classmates.

Library of Congress Cataloging-in-Publication Data
    Westhoven, Karen
    Good for You, Grisha! Teaching Kids Ways to Cope/Karen Westhoven – First Edition
    ISBN-13: 978-1938326-03-5
    1. Juvenile fiction. 2. Self-confidence. 3. Self-control. 4. Coping skills.
    I. Westhoven, Karen II. Title
    Library of Congress Control Number: 2012941721

FERNE PRESS

Ferne Press is an imprint of Nelson Publishing & Marketing
366 Welch Road, Northville, MI 48167
www.nelsonpublishingandmarketing.com
(248) 735-0418

I dedicate this book to my beloved family: Brad, Jess, and Greg.

I acknowledge all the teachers, parents, and those who work with children. This book is also for adoptive families and individuals who have struggles. I hope this book will help children overcome fears and learn how to cope with and handle daily struggles. Know you are not alone.

I sincerely thank Marian Nelson and Kris Yankee for their support and for believing in me and my vision to help others through literature.

It was Grisha's first day of school. He had butterflies in his stomach but couldn't wait for class to begin. When Grisha introduced himself to the class, a girl said, "That sounds funny! Where are you from?"

Grisha replied, "I was adopted from Russia."
Grisha started to feel uncomfortable.
"Don't feel bad," whispered a boy named David. "I was adopted, too."
"Wow, I thought I was the only one," Grisha said, feeling instantly better.

During a spelling test, Grisha got upset because he couldn't remember several words.
"I don't want to be the last to finish," he told Mrs. Miller.
"It doesn't matter if we finish first or last, Grisha. It's doing our best that matters," Mrs. Miller replied.

That didn't help, and Grisha lost his temper and started to cry.
"Please go to Principal Schroeder's office so you can calm down. The rest of the class needs to finish their test," said Mrs. Miller.

"Back again, Grisha?" asked the school secretary. "Principal Schroeder will be with you shortly."
"At least Principal Schroeder listens to me and helps me calm down," thought Grisha.

Grisha and Principal Schroeder discussed what had happened in class.

"I'm so tired of being slow," said Grisha.

"Each of us is unique in our own way," Principal Schroeder said.

"We all have struggles, some more than others. How we handle them is most important. Why did you lose control during your test? What are you supposed to do when you get upset?"

"I forgot my little turtle," replied Grisha. "I reached inside my pocket and he wasn't there. I got frustrated and couldn't relax. You know how my turtle makes me feel safe. I know I should take deep breaths and think of positive things, but right now, I could really use my turtle."

"I will give you my extra turtle to use today," said Principal Schroeder.
Grisha took the turtle, held it tightly for a second, and took a few deep breaths.
Smiling, Grisha said, "I'm ready to finish my test."
"Good job, Grisha!" said Principal Schroeder. "You know where I am if you need me."

During recess, the boys played football.

"That was the wrong play, Grisha! How many times do we have to tell you?" the team captain yelled.

"I didn't know that was the play you wanted to run!" Grisha yelled back. "Why can't I understand football like they do?" he wondered.

He stomped off toward the basketball court.

"Hey! We've got a big game coming up. Do you want to shoot some hoops with me?" David asked while dribbling a ball. "I was never into football anyway."
Grisha smiled and said, "Sounds good! Maybe with enough practice, our team will win."

Later that day, Grisha told his mom, "I feel like I'm the only one who has problems, and that will never change. It makes me very sad."
"Well, it couldn't have all been bad. Did anything good happen today?" Mom asked.

After a few minutes, Grisha said, "I shot hoops with David. He's the coolest kid in the class. We had fun and practiced a lot."

"That's wonderful," Mom replied. "Why don't you make a list of all the good things that happen each day so you don't forget? You can hang it on the refrigerator and look at it anytime."
"I guess we could do that," said Grisha.

"Always know, God and I love you for who you are and not for who you think you should be. You need to love yourself as well," said his mom. "Hopefully your list will help remind you how to do that. Now let's work on your spelling words."

In speech class, Alyssa whispered, "I'm not going to read out loud because I'm too slow and scared." Grisha replied, "I'm slow, too. Don't worry. Here, use my turtle. He helps me feel safe and strong." "Thanks," Alyssa replied.

Grasping the turtle, Alyssa took a deep breath and raised her hand to read. When she finished, Alyssa smiled and said, "That wasn't so bad!"

"I knew you could do it," Grisha said.

"Next time, you'll have to read out loud. If I can do it, you can, too," said Alyssa.

19

Over the next few days, Alyssa told many of their classmates about what had happened in speech class. "That turtle really helped me. I couldn't believe it! Miss Gray said that was my best reading yet! I think we all should have turtles like Grisha," stated Alyssa.

While getting ready for bed, Mom asked, "Anything good happen today?"

"Remember how my turtle and I helped Alyssa in speech class?" Grisha asked. "Now all the kids are asking me about it and how to get one. Do you think we can give a turtle to everyone?"

"That's a wonderful idea," said Mom. "I'll see what I can do."

The next day at the fifth and sixth grade basketball game, Grisha's team was losing and everyone's spirits were down.
"We have to help the team, David," Grisha said.
"We've practiced a lot."

Grisha played hard and even made a couple of baskets. Everyone watching clapped when he scored. Coach White said, "If we all play hard like Grisha and David, we might win!"
The team came back and won the game.

After the game, Grisha's teammates gave him high fives and patted him on the shoulder. "Awesome, Grisha!" they all said.

Coach White took the team out for ice cream and said, "Grisha, you are the most improved player on the team."
"Thanks, Coach. I always try to do my very best," Grisha said.

It was the last day of school and time for the year-end party. Grisha's mom appeared in the doorway with turtle-shaped cookies and a surprise for everyone.

"If you are ever upset, this might help," Grisha said as he handed one to each classmate.

"Thanks for all the turtles, Mom. Everyone likes them."
"I am so proud of you!" Grisha's mom said.

"Guess what? I didn't even have my turtle, and I still got a B+ on the final spelling test!"

My inspiration for this book is my son Grisha, or Gregory. Grisha is the child version of the Russian name Grigory. We adopted Greg from Russia in 2001, at the age of two. By the age of five, he was diagnosed with severe hypothyroidism, developmental delays, and fetal alcohol affects. Raising a special needs child is both inspiring and challenging. I immediately realized that a team of professionals was needed for Greg to succeed. Being a physician assistant, and a diligent mother, I was blessed to find a wonderful group of people to help Greg through each phase of his life and struggles. Not every family is as fortunate. I have seen this first hand with the special needs patients in my office.

One thing that is apparent with Greg, and other special needs children, is that they often believe they are the only ones that are different and that no one understands. They frequently fail to realize that every-one has struggles or problems to overcome. Helping children and giving them the confidence and tools necessary to succeed is paramount.

My hope is that this book will show all children they are not alone, especially those with special needs. Help can come from parents, teachers, coaches, and peers. The more support and coping mechanisms we teach our children, the better equipped they will be to face their life challenges.

Karen Westhoven is a physician assistant in family practice. She loves working with children of all ages, especially those with special needs. Karen lives in Napoleon, Ohio, with her husband, Brad, and two children, Greg and Jessica, who were adopted from Russia. She enjoys family and friends. Most important, she loves helping others.

For more information about Karen, please visit www.karenwesthovenbooks.com.

Mary Gregg Byrne lives in Bellingham, Washington. She reads, writes, and creates art. Mary teaches watercolor classes and illustrates children's books. She watches her garden and the children grow. She walks in the mountains. She cherishes her friends. Mary enjoys the changing light of the seasons and of her life.

For more information about Mary and her art, please visit www.marygreggbyrne.com.